Fun at Playtime

Based on the characters created by
Ellen Crimi-Trent

priddy books

For cousins Sid and Suzy Snail,
playtime was always the same.

Out in the playground,
Sid sat under the tree
with his book.

He noticed Suzy playing on her skateboard with her friends. It looked like fun! Just for today, he didn't feel like reading.

Suzy rolled around on her skateboard,
but she felt tired and wasn't having any fun.

Suzy spotted Sid reading his book. Just for today, she felt like sitting still.

Suzy rolled over to where Sid sat.
She looked at Sid's book.

Sid looked at Suzy's skateboard.

Suzy sighed. She wanted to be quiet and read a good book.

Sid sighed. He wanted to shout and play with the other Schoolies.

Quietly, Sid rolled over to where Spencer was roller skating. He felt nervous.

Hi!

But Spencer hadn't noticed Sid.
He was having too much fun!

Sid looked back at his favourite tree and his favourite book. He was unsure what to do.

Then Spencer spotted Sid, and soon enough,
Sid was having lots of fun rolling around, too.

Under the tree, Suzy watched Sid for a while.
She wondered if the Schoolies missed her.

Then she opened up the book
and started to read.

Suzy could hear the sounds of the Schoolies playing, but soon she was lost in her story.

Too soon, the bell rang for the end of playtime. **Brrring! Brrring!**

Just for today, it was fun to try something new.

Maybe they'd try something new again tomorrow.